The Norfin® Trolls
Camp-out Adventure

A Norfin® Troll Tale

by Karen Berman
Illustrated by Jill

SCHOLASTIC INC.
New York   Toronto   London   Auckland   Sydney

ISBN 0-590-46630-5

12 11 10 9 8 7 6 5 4 3 2 1   3 4 5 6 7 8/9

Printed in the U.S.A.   24

First Scholastic printing, April 1993

Summer was Bruce and Jimmy Troll's favorite time of year. And this summer Bruce and Jimmy were finally allowed to go on an overnight camp-out in the woods. But they could only go if their older sister Wendy went with them. The big problem was, Wendy did not want to go!

Bruce and Jimmy tried to get her to change her mind. "Please, Wendy, please," they begged. "Mom and Dad will never let us go alone!"

"You're the only one of us who can build a fire and set up a tent," Jimmy pleaded.

"And you know all about the great outdoors," Bruce said.

Her brothers were telling the truth. Wendy was a Troll Scout. She went camping all the time with her Troll Scout troop. She could row a boat, bait a hook, and tie three different kinds of knots. But Wendy never camped out at night without a grown-up along. She was scared, but she wouldn't let on to her brothers.

"I just don't want to go!" she snapped at them. Then she buried her head in her book.

Wendy didn't want to hurt her brothers. But she didn't know what to do. Maybe Beth can help, she thought.

Beth was Wendy's best friend and fellow Troll Scout. Wendy ran over to her house and told her about the camp-out.

"I can't go," Wendy cried. "There are all sorts of spooky things in the dark. I'm afraid. I've never slept out without grown-ups before. What should I do?"

Beth laughed. "There's nothing to be scared of, silly," she said. "Everything is the same at night as it is during the day — only it's dark. My Grandma Eleanor Troll used to say, 'You have nothing to fear but fear itself.'"

"Brilliant!" Wendy said angrily. "I bet your Grandma Troll never came face-to-face with a 10-foot monster or a wild grizzly bear in the dark. I bet she never spent the night outdoors without a grown-up. Thanks for nothing!"

Wendy stormed out and went home.

Bruce and Jimmy were waiting for her as she stomped up the walkway.

"Have you changed your mind? Will you go with us?" Jimmy called out.

"We'll make your bed every day for a month if you come," Bruce yelled.

"Please, Wendy," they both cried.

The boys had no idea Wendy was scared, and she didn't want them to find out. After all, she was supposed to be their big, brave sister — not a scaredy-cat.

"Okay, okay, I'll go," she sighed.

The day of the camp-out, the three of them packed their gear: pots and pans, sleeping bags, a tent, fishing poles, and food. They hugged their parents good-bye and off they went.

Deep into the woods they walked, with Wendy leading the way.

"What's that Wendy?" Bruce asked, pointing to a beautiful golden flower.

"That's a black-eyed Susan," she answered.

"What kind of a bird is that?" asked Jimmy, as a tiny bird flew by.

"A ruby-throated hummingbird," Wendy answered. "They can fly backwards!"

Wendy felt good. She *did* know a lot about nature and she liked teaching her younger brothers all she had learned.

Soon they picked a spot for their campsite. And Wendy helped Bruce and Jimmy set up the tent and roll out their sleeping bags. Then she said, "We're going to make a big campfire tonight. You stay here while I go look for firewood before it gets dark."

Wendy walked through the woods
gathering twigs and branches. Mockingbirds
sang and chipmunks scattered.

Suddenly everything seemed silent. Wendy stood still, listening. Then she heard the sound of twigs snapping and dried leaves crackling as footsteps walked over them.

"Hello!" she cried out. But no one answered.

As she bent down to pick up a branch, Bruce and Jimmy jumped out from behind a big tree.

"Boo! Boo!" they yelled.

Wendy screamed and raced to the campsite.
The boys followed, laughing all the way.
When they reached the campsite, Wendy pretended
that she wasn't frightened at all.
"I knew you were going to do that. I was just playing
along," she said and joined in laughing.

Afterward, they sat back and watched the sunset together. The sky was lit up with shades of purple and pink.

After a while their stomachs grumbled with hunger. So Wendy started a roaring fire and fixed a dinner of hot dogs and beans.

As the evening grew darker, the night noises began.

"*Hooot, hooot!*" they heard.

The brothers trembled. "That sounds like a ghost!" they said.

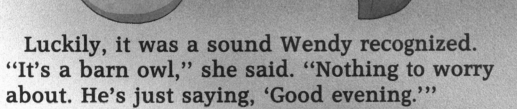

Luckily, it was a sound Wendy recognized. "It's a barn owl," she said. "Nothing to worry about. He's just saying, 'Good evening.'"

A few minutes later, a deep *CROAAAK* filled the air.

"What's that?" cried Jimmy and Bruce.

"That's a bullfrog looking for a wife," Wendy said.

Then she suddenly thought, What happens if there is a creepy sound that I can't explain?

Right before bedtime, Wendy reminded
her brothers to brush their teeth. With their
toothbrushes in hand, Bruce and Jimmy
went off to the brook, frowning and
grumbling all the way.

Wendy stayed behind at the campfire, brushing her long blue hair and counting each stroke. "...forty-one, forty-two, forty-three..."

Then *Snap! Crackle! Pop!* went the wood in the fire.

Wendy jumped up! She turned slowly toward the tent — and froze!

There in the moonlight by the tent, she saw a huge, dark, frightening figure with its arms raised high above its head!

"Jimmy? Bruce?" Wendy called out in a trembling voice. "Stop fooling around!"

But her brothers did not appear. Wendy was terrified. She wished there was a grown-up around. She stared at the frightening figure.

"A monster!" she murmured.

Then she shook her hands at it and, in a shaky voice, she yelled as loud as she could, "Go away! Get out of here!"

The monster did not leave. And there was still no sign of Bruce or Jimmy. Wendy had to face the monster alone. She told herself to be brave. Waving her arms frantically, she shooed the monster away again! But as she did, the monster just waved back at her!

"Oh!" she said. "It's making fun of me!" Wendy got really angry now — and bold. She inched closer to the tent — closer to the monster.

With each step closer to the monster, Wendy's heart beat louder — and faster. Suddenly, she stopped in her tracks!

This was no monster — it was her own shadow! She felt so silly. She doubled over laughing. Her shadow doubled over laughing, too.

Just then, the moon slipped behind a cloud and darkness surrounded Wendy. She felt a tap on her shoulder.

"Aiiieee!" she screamed.

"It's only me," said Beth, as she came around to face Wendy. "I didn't mean to scare you. I just thought you might need some company out here tonight."

Wendy hugged Beth tightly. "I'm so happy it's you!" she cried. "For a minute I thought it was a..."

"Monster?" Beth said.

The two friends laughed and laughed.

"Hey, where did *you* come from?" Jimmy said to Beth, as the brothers returned to the campsite.

"And what's so funny?" asked Bruce.

Neither one waited for an answer.

They were eager to start the campfire.

Finally the four campers settled down around the blazing campfire, roasting marshmallows. Wendy looked around and noticed how bright the night was. Many stars dotted the sky. The moon shone over them. The fire burned brightly.

Wendy wasn't frightened anymore.

She was glad Beth was there, but she didn't need her. She knew the nighttime wasn't scary. It was only her fear that made her afraid of the dark.

"Hey, guys, it's scary story time," said Beth. "Who's got a good story to tell?"

"I do, I do!" cried Wendy.

Before she began her story, Wendy turned to her brothers. "Hey, guys, when's our next camping trip?" she asked as she popped another marshmallow in her mouth.